# What Does the Rooster Say, Yoshio?

Story by EDITH BATTLES

Pictures by TONI HORMANN

ALBERT WHITMAN & Company, Chicago

PLAY FARM

TEXT © COPYRIGHT 1978 BY EDITH BATTLES. ILLUSTRATIONS © COPYRIGHT 1978 by TONI HORMANN
PUBLISHED SIMULTANEOUSLY IN CANADA BY GEORGE J. McLEOD, LIMITED, TORONTO. PRINTED IN U.S.A.
CIP INFORMATION IN BACK

こんにちわ

In Japan, Yoshio could talk to everyone.

But here, he could not talk to anyone he met.

Yoshio could not talk to Lynn.
So he talked to the animals.

"Wan, wan!" he said to the dog.

ワン ワン

Lynn said, "Bowwow! Bowwow!"

Bowwow!

"Wan, wan!" said Yoshio.
"Bowwow!" said Lynn.

So Yoshio stamped his foot
and walked away.

Yoshio saw the ducks.
He talked to them.
"Ga, ga!" he said.

ガァー　ガァー

"Quack, quack!" said Lynn.

"Ga, ga!" said Yoshio.

A sparrow hopped along.
Yoshio said, "Choon, choon."

"Cheep, cheep," said Lynn.

ヒヒィーン

Yoshio saw a horse.
He liked horses.

"He-heen, he-heen," he said.

Lynn said, "Neigh, neigh."

"Neigh?" asked Yoshio.
He gave the horse an apple.

Yoshio stopped in front of the sheep.
He looked at Lynn.
He did not say anything.

"Baa, baa," she said.

"May, may," Yoshio told her.

Oink, oink!　ブーブー

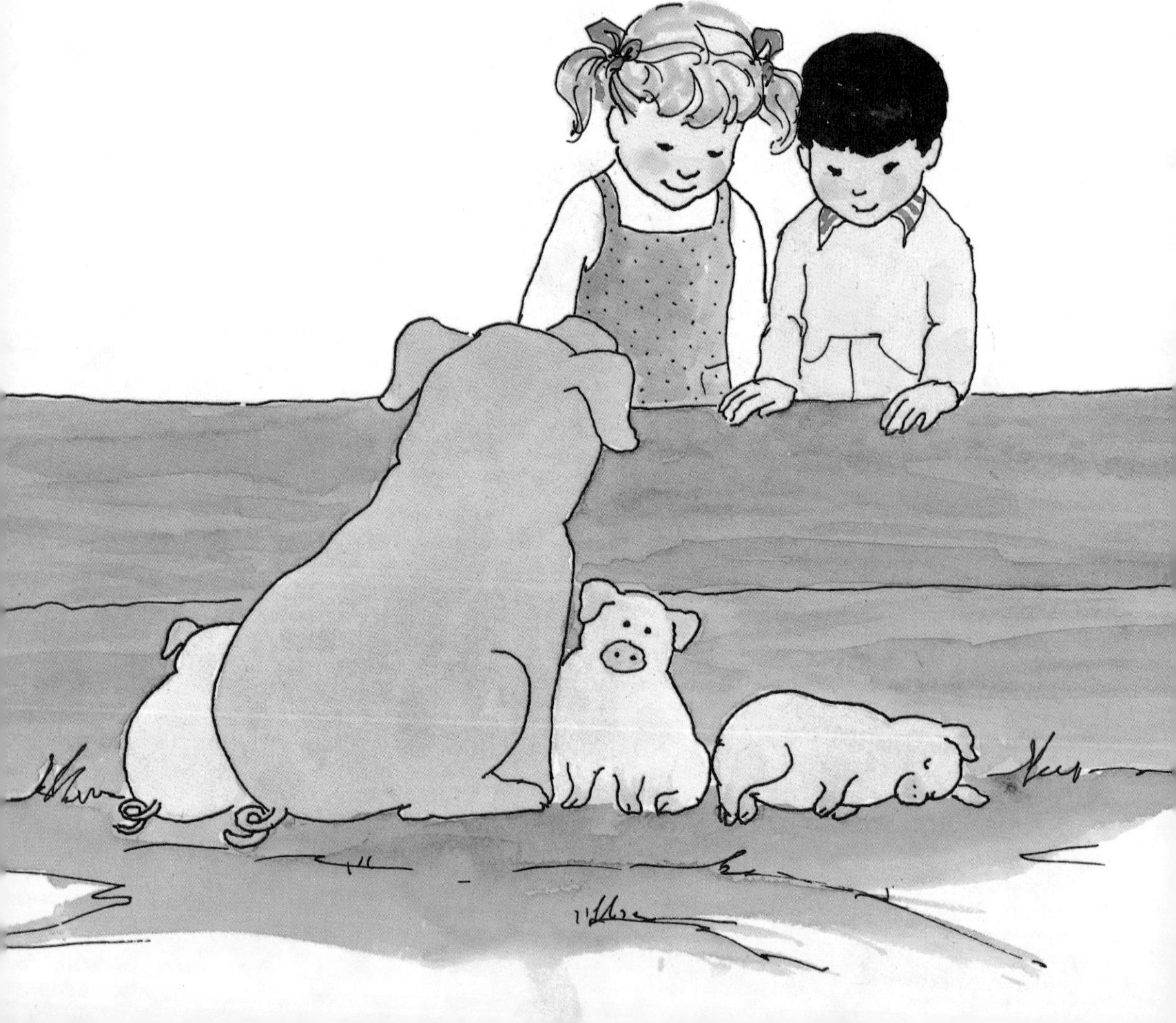

Now they saw some pigs.
Yoshio and Lynn looked at each other.

"Oink, oink," said Lynn.

"Bu, bu," said Yoshio.
Then he asked, "Oink, oink?"

"Oink, oink," said Lynn.
And then she tried saying "Bu, bu."

コケコッコー

A rooster was next.
Lynn looked at Yoshio.

"Ko-kay-ko-ko!" said Yoshio.

"Ko-kay-ko-ko?" asked Lynn.

Yoshio looked at Lynn.
"Cock-a-doodle-doo!" she said.

"Cock-a-doodle-doo?" he asked.
Then he laughed—
"Cock-a-doodle-doo!"

Yoshio and Lynn saw a cow.
They looked at each other.

At the very same time,
they both said, "Moo!"
    Just like that—"Moo!"

And the cow said, "Moo," too.

So Yoshio and Lynn skipped back
to their mothers, saying
"MOO!" all the way.

## About the Author

Picture books by Edith Battles, like her *One to Teeter-totter*, have been translated into other languages and published abroad. This set Mrs. Battles to thinking. And, since she is an elementary teacher in California as well as an author, she looked and listened to youngsters in her school. What she saw was a mixture of children from different lands and what she heard was a variety of languages.

In this age of global travel and business, many families come to the United States, and their children enter school. Why not, Mrs. Battles thought, write a story in which children who speak different languages meet and learn from each other? Thus the stage was set for Yoshio, fresh from Japan, to overcome frustration and succeed in communicating with a new friend. It began when Yoshio talked in Japanese to the farm animals in a park. He and a little girl discover that both agree the cow says moo, and so understanding commences.

Library of Congress Cataloging in Publication Data
Battles, Edith.
   What does the rooster say, Yoshio?
   (Self-starter books)
   SUMMARY: A Japanese boy and an American girl comparing the sounds of the animals in their own languages find one animal that says the same thing to both of them.
   [1. Animal sounds—Fiction. 2. Japanese language—Fiction] I. Hormann, Toni. II. Title.
PZ7.B3246Wh          [E]          78-12824
ISBN 0-8075-3628-8